A Note to Parents and Caregivers:

Read-it! Readers are for children who are just starting on the amazing road to reading. These beautiful books support both the acquisition of reading skills and the love of books.

 The PURPLE LEVEL presents basic topics and objects using high frequency words and simple language patterns.

 The RED LEVEL presents familiar topics using common words and repeating sentence patterns.

 The BLUE LEVEL presents new ideas using a larger vocabulary and varied sentence structure.

 The YELLOW LEVEL presents more challenging ideas, a broad vocabulary, and wide variety in sentence structure.

 The GREEN LEVEL presents more complex ideas, an extended vocabulary range, and expanded language structures.

 The ORANGE LEVEL presents a wide range of ideas and concepts using challenging vocabulary and complex language structures.

When sharing a book with your child, read in short stretches, pausing often to talk about the pictures. Have your child turn the pages and point to the pictures and familiar words. And be sure to reread favorite stories or parts of stories.

There is no right or wrong way to share books with children. Find time to read with your child, and pass on the legacy of literacy.

Adria F. Klein, Ph.D.
Professor Emeritus
California State University
San Bernardino, California

Editor: Christianne Jones
Designer: Nathan Gassman
Page Production: Tracy Kaehler
Creative Director: Keith Griffin
Editorial Director: Carol Jones
The illustrations in this book were created digitally.

Picture Window Books
5115 Excelsior Boulevard
Suite 232
Minneapolis, MN 55416
877-845-8392
www.picturewindowbooks.com

Printed in the United States of America.

Library of Congress Cataloging-in-Publication Data
Anderson, Joseph P., 1982-
Loop, swoop, and pull! / [written and] illustrated by Joseph P. Anderson.
p. cm. — (Read-it! readers)
Summary: Stevie practices tying his shoes and receives the satisfaction of a job
well done.
ISBN 1-4048-1611-9 (hardcover)
[1. Shoes—Fiction. 2. Shoelaces—Fiction.] I. Title. II. Series.

PZ7.A5376Loo 2005
[E]—dc22   2005021447

Loop, Swoop, and Pull!

written and illustrated by
Joseph P. Anderson

Special thanks to our advisers for their expertise:

Adria F. Klein, Ph.D.
Professor Emeritus, California State University
San Bernardino, California

Susan Kesselring, M.A.
Literacy Educator
Rosemount–Apple Valley–Eagan (Minnesota) School District

PICTURE WINDOW BOOKS
Minneapolis, Minnesota

"Stevie, it's time to get up," my mom said.

4

Today is the big day. Today, my mom is going to teach me how to tie my shoes.

I put on my red shoes. They have bright white laces.

"OK, Stevie, just watch and listen,"
my mom said.

"Start by crossing the laces.

8

Tuck one lace under the other,
and pull it tight."

"Next, make a loop with one lace.
Swoop the other lace around the loop."

"Then, after you swoop, pull the lace through the hole to make another loop. Pull each loop tight."

"Now, say it with me:
Loop, swoop, and pull!"

I didn't get it right away.
I kept practicing.

I practiced all weekend.

16

I couldn't think of anything else.
Loop, swoop, and pull!

Before school on Monday, I put my shoes on.

Loop, swoop, and pull! I tied my shoe!

I was so proud of myself. I showed my mom, my cat, my goldfish, and my friends.

I tied my own shoes, and so can you.
Just remember these words:
Loop, swoop, and pull!

More *Read-it!* Readers

Bright pictures and fun stories help you practice your reading skills. Look for more books at your level.

Bamboo at the Beach 1-4048-1035-8

The Best Lunch 1-4048-1578-3

Clinks the Robot 1-4048-1579-1

The Crying Princess 1-4048-0053-0

Eight Enormous Elephants 1-4048-0054-9

Flynn Flies High 1-4048-0563-X

Freddie's Fears 1-4048-0056-5

Marvin, the Blue Pig 1-4048-0564-8

Mary and the Fairy 1-4048-0066-2

Megan Has to Move 1-4048-1613-5

Moo! 1-4048-0643-1

My Favorite Monster 1-4048-1029-3

Pippin's Big Jump 1-4048-0555-9

Pony Party 1-4048-1612-7

The Queen's Dragon 1-4048-0553-2

Sounds Like Fun 1-4048-0649-0

Tired of Waiting 1-4048-0650-4

Whose Birthday Is It? 1-4048-0554-0

Looking for a specific title or level? A complete list of *Read-it!* Readers is available on our Web site:
www.picturewindowbooks.com

24